Submitting to the Dominatrix

A Cuckold's Sexual Awakening

Amber Carden

Chapter 1: The Invitation 3

Chapter 2: The First Encounter 19

Chapter 3: The Turning Point 37

Chapter 4: Embracing Change 55

Chapter 5: Re-evaluating Boundaries 69

Chapter 1: The Invitation

Ava

"Met Marcus for lunch, didn't you?"

Ethan's voice, smooth as silk, sends a shiver down my spine as his fingers trace what I know must be a faint bruise on my neck.

My heart pounds as I realize in my hurry, I forgot to apply concealer. A hint of guilt pricks my insides.

Slowly, his fingers curl at the back of my neck, pulling me into a kiss—gentle, possessive, erasing traces of another from my lips.

"Enjoyed it?" he breathes in my ear, placing a quick kiss. I'm unsure if he's referring to our kiss or what he thinks happened with

Marcus. The valet brings Ethan's Mercedes, sparing me from answering.

The leather seats warmed by the sun feel great against the skin. I stretch my legs while Ethan sets the navigation for D'Armonde Muse, an art gallery forty minutes away in New York. His faint cologne lingers in the car, soothing my frayed nerves.

"Do you think we'll get in?" I ask, glancing at the road ahead, running my fingers through my hair, removing invisible knots.

"Who knows?" Ethan's grip tightens slightly on the wheel, his eyes focused on the traffic. "Blaze said they're quite selective. Most applicants are rejected over chats. We got the meeting."

I nod, a smile tugging at my lips. "I have a good feeling about this." The idea of exploring partners outside of Westchester has me buzzing from within—an exciting change from our usual routine.

He rubs my thigh, offering a brief, bright smile before returning his attention to the highway.

"Leon's Grotto," I murmur, watching the signs zip past. "An unusual name for a swingers club, isn't it?"

"Sounds like a statutory warning to me. Be prepared for consequences when you walk into a lion's den." His laugh breaks the tension, and I can't help but hit his arm playfully.

"I meant it gives an exotic, luxurious vibe. That's why I got my favorite black dress out. My date couldn't…"

His eyes flick over to me, a brief glance that makes my insides clench. I realize my mistake.

"Uhm… Marcus was out of town, so I thought I'd meet with this other guy while I waited for you. It was just lunch." My voice trembles slightly as I avoid his gaze. I can feel the heat creeping up my neck, a telltale sign of my deception.

His eyes harden for a brief moment before softening. He knows the truth; he always does. I've just avoided saying it because it hurts him. The unspoken agreement between us is fragile, a delicate balance of trust and boundaries.

His hand, resting on my thigh, tightens imperceptibly. I can almost sense the silent battle within him. I lean in and gently hug his arm. "It's crazy how skewed the gender ratio is on these apps. Maybe if this swingers club works, it could be something we both can enjoy—together."

He takes a deep breath before letting out a little hum. "I got our STD panel results. Everything checks out. At least we can't be rejected on those grounds."

"Ah, okay. Cool." I let out a relieved sigh, seeing his shoulders relax. "Blaze said it's completely anonymous, so our identities are protected."

"Yeah, protected from everyone else except the owners since they'll see our details on the blood work," he says, a hint of skepticism in his tone.

"Want to regroup on the expected questions?"

He keeps his eyes on the road, the corners of his mouth twitching slightly. "I don't think we would've been friends in school."

He glances at me again and his wide smile puts me at ease.

"C'mon, we still have a few minutes before we arrive." Clearing my throat, I ask, "Kinks you want to explore?"

"I haven't really thought about it," he shrugs.

"Hold on," I pause, considering my words. "How about, 'We're open to exploring'?"

He shakes his head. "I'd bet ten dollars you were always the teacher's pet."

I laugh and don't deny it. "Okay, I got another one. 'Are you both in it consensually? We don't want anyone being forced into things or someone bringing our club as grounds for divorce.'"

"Absolutely consensual," he says bringing the car to a halt. "Together for eleven years, married for eight, open for almost a year now. We both love to explore."

While he hands over the keys to the valet, I check my makeup in the rear-view mirror and dab another hint of perfume on my pulse points. There's been a subtle distance growing between us lately, and I'm hoping getting into Leon's Grotto will reignite the spark between us.

Ethan kisses my cheek and grabs my arm, whispering "Beautiful" in my ear as we head in, making me hopeful that he feels it too.

Nestled amidst high-end boutiques and restaurants, the gallery's understated limestone exterior is marked only by a discreet gold-embossed 88. We might have missed it if not for the uniformed doorman with the gallery name embroidered on the chest.

Inside is a different story. Towering ceilings, pristine white walls adorned with vibrant canvases, and a subtle pine fragrance fill the air. Soft jazz music mingles with hushed conversations.

Ethan and I exchange a silent smile as we are guided through a narrow passage to the private viewing room at the back.

His fingers briefly flick mine before the heavy door opens. Standing by the massive French windows is a stunning couple.

I don't even realize holding my breath for a moment.

When our old friend Blaze, a former club member, had described the selection process, I'd pictured someone older. These guys look barely out of their twenties.

He's all sun-kissed hair, intense eyes, and lean muscle. She's a knockout with piercing green eyes, full lips, and a killer body. Together they look straight out of The Hollywood Reporter's front cover. There's a glow about them.

The man smiles, his eyes twinkling with amusement as he gestures towards the couches.

As Ethan and I approach, I notice how the man's gaze never strays from who I assume is his wife. There's a sense of deep affection and perhaps an underlying tension.

"Hi! I'm Julian," he says, leaning back on the couch. "And this is Vanessa."

"I'm Ethan and this is my gorgeous wife, Ava. She is the one who exchanged messages with you." Ethan's voice cracks slightly as he introduces me, and his hand, clammy and cold, grabs mine, intertwining our fingers.

Vanessa, nods at us, her eyes holding a challenge. Her grip is tight on Julian's arm.

"We've heard a lot about the club and would love to be a part of it," I add, wanting to express our enthusiasm.

Vanessa's lips curve into a knowing smile. "I'm glad you decided to join us."

I straighten my back mentally preparing myself for their questions.

"So, let's get to the essentials," Vanessa begins, her voice husky. "To clear a few common misconceptions, this isn't your traditional couple swapping with one another. This is an experience. Think of it as…," she pauses, her gaze flits from us to the calla-lilies on the table before adding, "…a holiday. But with a bunch of people who love sex."

I sense my husband's excitement without even looking at him. It's in the way his fingers move around mine. But while Ethan and I might be able to write a song on how good they look, I'm unsure how they see us as they tell us about the club.

"We choose the venue, set the scene, and unite like-minded people. That's all. You decide what you want to do. You can still choose to only be with your partner or play individually. You can do traditional swaps with another couple or play with multiple partners at the same time. We love for people to explore."

I glance at Ethan, who nods in understanding. "Uhm… so how many people will be there?" I ask, trying to keep the tremor off my voice.

Julian responds, "Twenty couples, meaning forty people including Vanessa and me."

Forty people? My mind immediately conjures up a scenario of an orgy something I've never been to.

"We value everyone's safety and privacy, which is why it's all anonymous and dynamic. No fixed dates, no set locations. Each time we play, it's in a new venue."

"You mean like a pop-up?" I blurt out.

Vanessa laughs softly, her gaze drifting to Ethan. "Something like that. It keeps things exciting and unpredictable."

Julian's eyes meet mine. "It can be intense, but it's also liberating. Trust is a big part of this. We expect everyone to play responsibly, but you are responsible for the safety of your partner. We have staff, security, and a doctor on call, but not on the premises. There are no cameras on the property either, so everyone can be free."

Ethan shakes his head. "Things can always be sneaked in." As I squeeze his palm, he adds, "I don't mean us. I was talking about others."

The gorgeous man grins, revealing a perfect line of teeth. I get a feeling he is amused by the two of us as he answers. "The only thing you're allowed to bring with you is yourselves. Not even your underwear. We provide you with towels, bathrobes, slippers—everything else stays in your car."

"Not even condoms?" my smarty pants husband pipes up.

"That'll all be available at the front desk. Same goes for food and drinks, you can order in. Everything is charged to your card."

It suddenly hits me that there have been no questions till now. These guys have straight come to rules. What does it mean? Are we in?

While Julian adds to the list of rules, I squeeze Ethan's fingers.

"We do not appreciate anyone getting drunk. No drugs at the venue. No coercion. No fights. These are grounds for immediate termination and ejection from the property.

You can take a look at the rest of the rules when you're signing the NDA. I'll have my assistant bring it over."

Ethan finally gets the idea and turns to me, both of us processing the information before turning to the couple.

Vanessa chuckles, "Of course you both are in. We like the dynamic you bring in."

I'm not sure what she means by 'dynamic' but I ignore it. I'm too busy doing a mental dance. We. Are. In.

This is going to change everything for us. I just know it.

Neither of us reacts immediately. Only once we are out and alone in the car, a block away from the gallery, do I notice the strain on Ethan's pants. Is it excitement, or did Vanessa catch his eye? Either way, I want to scream.

As our eyes meet, we both start laughing like kids.

"Can you believe this?" I gasp, my breath catching in my throat as the car screeches to a halt at the red light. Ethan's grin is infectious.

"Not until I signed that NDA," he replies, stealing a quick kiss before the impatient honk behind us forces him back to the road.

"You getting the tests done in advance was such a cool move. I think even they were impressed," I gush, rubbing his thigh. It's the reason we've been invited to the next 'play date' over the weekend.

His gaze flickers to me, the pin moving faster on the speedometer dial.

"We have to celebrate," I say, grinning, thinking of things we could do.

He chuckles, "And we shall."

The drive back home takes only twenty minutes and the moment the garage door shuts, we are on each other. Buttons flying, hands everywhere, lips frantic, my legs around his waist.

We are halfway over to the bedroom when Ethan halts. "Didn't you have plans for tonight?" His grip around me loosens.

"Already canceled," I tell him between kisses to his face. "I want to spend this time with you."

This time when he kisses me, I know we'll be up for a lot longer tonight.

Late at night while we're still tangled in the sheets, Ethan's body covering mine from behind, he suddenly asks, "Did you notice how Julian barely looked away from you during the meeting?"

"Umm... not really," I reply, trying to sound casual, but I sense his body tensing behind me so I turn to him, my finger poking him in the chest, teasing. "Although now that we're talking, Vanessa's gaze never strayed from you."

"Do you think he's taken a fancy to you?" he asks, his voice hiding what I see in his eyes–doubt. "Maybe it's why he approved us."

I reach over, tracing a finger along his jawline. "He literally has the most gorgeous woman beside him. And, anyway, this is about us exploring. And if Vanessa makes a move on you, I'd be thrilled for you. I want us to enjoy this."

I say that to him knowing that's never going to happen but a hint of a doubt flickers inside. When we opened our marriage, we'd made rules that we never talk about who we fuck, no one brings any dates over. Now for the first time, we'll be in the same space, with the same set of people–exploring.

With the weekend fast approaching, I know the possibilities are both thrilling and terrifying.

Chapter 2: The First Encounter

Ethan

My grip on Ava's waist tightens as she circles her hip over my cock once again making me want to reverse our positions but we're in a tight space and the steering wheel is right behind her back.

I tug at her hair, pulling her in for a kiss. The taste of the strawberry mint that she had been sucking on, mingling with her cherry lip balm is intoxicating.

The fact that we are just a lane away from a major interstate highway and can be seen by anyone has us hurrying. The thrill of being caught–heady.

As she rolls her hips again, I push her singlet and her bra up just above her chest, taking one of her pebbled nipples in my mouth.

She immediately starts clenching around me, making me throb. I know she is close.

Grabbing hold of her hips tight, I help her improve her rhythm as she starts to ride me hard.

Her wetness accentuates the sound of skin slapping each time I pull her down, her ass smacking against my balls. My full eight inches pulsing inside her and with her soft round tits bouncing right in my face, I'm racing to my peak.

I squeeze her ass tight and her movements become sloppy.

"Ah fuck."

Her strangled scream pushes me over the edge, my vision blurs, and I cum with a loud grunt. She flops onto me. Her tits squished into my chest, our breathing labored.

"Fuck! That was good."

We both take a minute to catch our breath before she moves back to her seat.

"God! Why didn't we ever do this before?" she asks as I'm handing over a few Kleenex to her while fixing my clothes.

She can't stop smiling. Neither can I. We could've easily been arrested.

"'Coz we've never driven to a sex party before," I reply as I get the engine running.

Less than a minute later a police car drives by.

"Holy shit!" I whisper under my breath.

Ava giggles, the sound infectious. "It's a sign," she says, running her fingers through my hair. "I think we're going to have a great time."

The rest of the drive flies by as Ava fields a call from her boss. Some nitpicky campaign details, I gather. I don't mind. It's early autumn and the drive to Summit is beautiful. I crack open a window, letting the crisp air in. Perfect driving weather. My mind goes back to our conversation last night.

"How do you wanna play this? Start with a normal swap but in the same room or different rooms. Do we join a group? Or maybe start with a threesome?"

I had brushed aside Ava's question last night with a simplistic, *"Let's play it by the ear."*

The truth is that while I'm excited, I don't want to rush into things. I want to savor the experience and see where the night takes us. I also don't want to look like an absolute rookie.

The reality is Ava and I are each other's firsts. And since opening our marriage she has had plenty of experience outside of me. I haven't.

As we round the final bend towards the Google pin, a mansion looms large. Someone clearly has access to obscene wealth.

The property is vast, its grounds easily worth a small fortune.

We're stopped by the iron gates while security checks our phones and faces before granting entry. Ava's grip tightens as we glide past manicured gardens, multiple greenhouses, and an Olympic-sized pool.

This place sure is something.

We're led into a nondescript outhouse where we strip down.

While we slip into the provided bathrobes, there's a strange excitement buzzing inside me. I'm not sure if it is to reassure her or myself, I whisper a soft 'I love you' as I kiss her on top of her head right before we step out.

There are some flower garlands placed in a basket with 'pick me' written on a card above it.

I throw one around Ava's neck. She giggles and throws one around mine and rolls one around her wrist like a bangle before we step away.

I don't see too many people around, but as we walk through the gardens, we hear music up ahead in the distance. The sky is swiftly getting dark and soft lights are hanging around.

A few steps ahead we take in the scene.

Multiple big HD screens are placed around. Each plays racy videos on mute. Lively music floating around–I'm guessing a pre-recorded DJ set. Dozen odd people are on the scene. No sign of Julian or Vanessa.

Bodies of different shapes, sizes, and colors are around. Everyone is either with a towel around their waist or naked.

There's a makeshift bar with champagne bottles in ice buckets and some other alcohol with mixers.

Ava looks around at the bathrobes and murmurs, "What do we do?"

"Whatever you're comfortable with, Ava" I reply, shrugging off my bathrobe and grabbing a towel from a nearby pile. "Want a drink?"

"Sure, wine sounds good, Frank," she says, glancing at the beverage counter before winking at me.

Ava and I chose Frank and Ava as our anon names. It's an iconic couple so no one would guess Ava is her real name.

I head over to the counter and get us both a glass of sparkling wine. As I return, I find Ava deep in conversation with another couple. Her bathrobe is off, and she's not bothering with a towel.

I introduce myself, "Hey, I'm Frank. Looks like you've been coming here for a while."

"Hi! I'm Butch and this is my wife, Cassidy," he says, grinning at the woman in his arms. They both seem to be in their early forties. "We couldn't have missed it since it's happening after six months."

Six months? Ava and I exchange a glance and grin. We sure did catch a lucky break.

The couple introduces us to others in the group, and mingling happens completely organically. I notice several people checking us out, clearly intrigued since Ava and I are the fresh arrivals.

Ava grabs my fingers and pulls me close. "Babe, I need the restroom. Can you refresh my drink till then?"

I take the empty glass from her with a smile. "Sure. I'll be right here."

While Ava walks away, Butch and Cassidy decide to share anecdotes from previous 'holidays' with the club, including a time when everyone indulged in a mass masturbation act.

"I mean, it was wild," Butch says with a laugh. "Everyone just let loose."

Cassidy chimes in, her voice low and teasing, "It was a real experience. You'd be surprised how liberating it is."

I move past the humor of their anonymous names and wonder if I would be open to that act. Cassidy's arm slings around my waist, her double D tits pressed into my sides. They feel quite firm, and I wonder if they are real. I've never felt up fake tits before.

Another couple walks over, and Cassidy leans in to whisper, "They've indulged together several times. You might find that interesting."

My towel is tenting in front of me. I can't wait to indulge.

I look around and notice Ava still isn't back. Her sparkling wine isn't bubbling as much as it was when I got it. She's been gone for more than twenty minutes.

I excuse myself and walk around, wondering if she's talking to someone else. I circle the entire area that's lit up but there's no sign of her.

I ask my way around to the bathrooms and she isn't there either.

There's no way to contact her since there are no phones.

As I'm walking past one of the private rooms, I hear soft moans, followed by a throaty groan.

"Damn! You're tight."

I smile. People are already indulging.

But then I hear a sound that makes my blood run cold. It's a giggle I've heard a million times over.

My eyes widen, and my heart hammers against my ribs.

I shake my head, trying to convince myself it can't be her. My insides shrivel up as a cold dread washes over me.

I want to walk away, but a morbid curiosity drives me to take a few steps closer. My feet halt right by the door. The scene in front of me sears my insides.

My wife Ava is on her fours, her face contorted in pain as her body moves rhythmically. Her eyes closed, her mouth open. Moans, and whimpers escaping her.

There's a bald man lined up behind her, pounding into her, with slow, hard thrusts, and right behind him is another woman with a strap-on plastered around her hips, slowly prodding his ass.

The scene is surreal. My eyes are fixated on the pink condom-covered cock, glistening, sliding in and out of Ava.

The movements of the woman at the back are deliberate and calculated. "That's it, take it all," she encourages and I notice the thick strap-on dildo is now fully inside the man's ass.

Their thrusts slowly get synced.

My mind is not able to understand what exactly is happening.

Ava's moans guiding the other two. Beads of sweat coating her back.

Was this what she wanted? Was the door left open for me to come and catch her?

I swallow the hurt and force myself to stare at the scene. If she wants me to watch her getting fucked then I shall.

The man's hands are gripping Ava's hips more for his support since the woman pegging him is getting into a faster rhythm.

I don't know if I make a sound but suddenly Ava's eyes clap onto mine and she whispers "shit!"

A flicker of shame crosses her face. "Eth, I…"

The man behind her continues to pound into her. The woman's pace behind him picking up.

I cut her off with a harsh tone. "Finish."

Her expression hardens, but she nods and continues.

The bald man grips her hips tighter and seems ready to burst. "That's it, baby. Give it to me harder," he says, his voice rough with need. The woman behind him presses closer, her voice low and encouraging. "You're doing great, Ava. Just a little more."

The scent of sex is heavy in the air.

Ava's body is shuddering with each thrust. Her moans grow louder, mingling with the grunts of her partners. She seems lost in the moment. Her back arches and starts gasping for breath. Her eyes though, keep flickering at me every now and then.

She wants to make sure I'm watching.

I stand there, feeling the sting of every sound and sight, unable to tear my eyes away. The sight of her in such raw abandon, completely immersed in the experience, only deepens the ache inside me.

Ava comes with a silent scream. The man pulls out of her, gets rid of the condom, and finishes with his hand.

I keep my eyes on my wife.

Her face has a soft, contented smile. There's no sign of regret on her face.

I step out of the room and head to the pool, needing space to process what I just saw.

"Are you angry with me, Eth?" Ava saunters over to me in her own sweet time. Her question makes me shake my head and I don't dignify it with a response.

"We agreed on this, Eth, didn't we?" Exhaling a sharp breath, she clamps her fingers on her waist. The same place where he had initially held her. "I thought we were here to explore."

I look at her, feeling the bite of her words but keep my face blank. "Fine, if that's how we roll. I've got my hall pass to indulge alone too."

The faintest of smiles crosses her lips before she turns and walks away.

I suddenly feel small. She thinks I have no game. Or maybe she is the one carrying the two of us here.

I yank the towel off my waist and throw it as far as I can, seething. I should've let them see—I'm bigger and thicker than that baldie.

"Fuck!"

I grab the railing in front, my grip slowly tightening, knuckles white with anger.

Sucking in deep breaths I try to cool down but then, something shifts. The air grows thick with the scent of lavender, and I feel a presence behind me.

"Party for one, is it?"

The husky voice has me straightening up instantly.

Goosebumps rise on my skin as soft fingers trail from my shoulder blades to my back. My insides thicken as her fingers continue their teasing path.

No way! It can't be Vanessa.

"I thought you wanted to explore," she teases, her voice dripping sensuality and my cock jerks back to life.

Her fingers draw circles over my ass before cupping it. Her nails digging in, causing a sting.

I turn to find her wearing a black lingerie. Not the lacy kind Ava wears but this one seems more like leather. It's hard and shiny, with straps and buckles crisscrossing her body.

But her tits are bare and they are lush.

The pink buds pebbled.

Damn it! Just the sight has my cock twitching.

"Ever been with a woman who likes to take charge?"

I try to focus on the question but the sight of her plump lips inches away from mine distracts me. Her warm breath hits my face.

She brings her thumb to run over my lips. "Tell me, ever been with a dominatrix?"

I blink. I've seen Fifty Shades and some dom-sub porn so I know the basic concept. But I'm not sure if I'm a submissive.

"It means I tell you what to do–in bed and outside. I know a lot of men aren't up for it."

I gaze into her eyes as I answer. "It depends whether the couple has chemistry."

She smirks before slowly running a nail over my nipple, almost scraping it. The touch sends a shockwave right to my throbbing cock. I gasp at the sensation and she chuckles.

"Have you always been this logical or for once would you just like to explore? No questions asked."

She leans in closer. Her lips a breath away from mine.

"If you do as I say, who knows I might let this see some action."

She gently taps the head of my cock before turning around and walking away.

"I'll be at the club room right across the pool entrance," she says when she's a few feet away.

What do I do? I've never been with a dominant woman before. I don't want to make a fool of myself again.

I palm my cock just to know things are real, before glancing at Vanessa's retreating figure.

I need to do this.

Chapter 3: The Turning Point

Ethan

Ten minutes. That's how long I've been standing inside this clubhouse–naked. My heart pounding a relentless rhythm but there's no sign of Vanessa.

I've scanned every inch of this room and the adjoining bathroom to know there's no camera or anyone else waiting to pounce on me.

Running my fingers through my hair for the hundredth time, I try to shake off the tension coiling in my gut.

Where the hell is she?

The room's almost empty. A gigantic bed, an upholstered ottoman, a wooden footstool, and one small lightbulb. The light is dim but I can make out that no effort has been made into this 'clubhouse' decor. The walls are bare and the cement flooring is cold under the feet. Not a single window in the room.

A strong scent lingers in the air. Pine, maybe. It reminds me of the art gallery where we first met Vanessa and her husband.

Click. Clack. Click. Clack.

The sound of heels echoing off the cement floor is sharp and my breath catches. The lavender lingers in the air again.

I turn to find her piercing gaze locked on me. A barely-there smile grazing her lips. "Good decision," she says, her voice sharp.

As she steps closer to me, I'm entranced by the little tremors in her tits with each movement. Her nipples, more prominent than Ava's, make me imagine the feel of them against my tongue.

Her stomach is flat and tight, a diamond glinting from her belly button piercing.

Just as I'm about to let my gaze drop lower, she suddenly produces a whip, holding it just under my chin and gently pushing my face up.

"Not so fast. I need you to shower first." She takes the whip off my chin and points to the bathroom. "Get in."

The thrill that's coursing my body is indescribable. Her eyes are only on me. Her attention fixed on my actions.

I'm about to turn the shower head on when she says, "Hold on, I need you to empty your bladder first."

My eyes widen in surprise. I turn to her, frowning, and see her casually palming one of her tits, her fingers running over her nipple, twisting it.

I don't waste a moment in standing over the commode, holding my hard cock in my hand. I try to relax, but nothing happens. I know her eyes are on me.

A wave of humiliation washes over me as I stand there, trying to squeeze the liquid out of me.

I take a few deep breaths, stroking myself. Let it go. Do it.

I roll the skin back and forth, applying pressure until, slowly a drop trickles out. It's the sound of her sigh that finally triggers the flow and the whole thing comes out gushing.

I turn to find her leaning against the door, sipping wine. She nods at me. "Good. Now shower."

I try the lever on both sides but there's only cold water. The damn thing shocks my system but I soap every inch and try to be quick. I want more time with her.

When I step out, she points me to the footstool and I go take a seat. She walks over to me and stand right in front, less than a foot away from me. Her core is perfectly lined in front of my face. Between the criss-cross leather, I realize she is bare.

My heartbeats pick up as I try to breathe her in from a distance. But then she slowly lifts one of her legs, placing it on the upper edge of the ottoman next to me.

I freeze for a moment.

"You'll follow my instructions, and if you don't like it, you can tap out. We end this experience right then. Clear?"

I hear her voice but my eyes are on her cunt. Despite the low light, I can see the pink bundle of nerves playing peekaboo between the smooth lips that are parted. Fuck! The sight is beautiful.

"I'd like an answer," she says.

"Yes, I understand."

She takes her leg down and grabbing my hand, pulls me to my feet. "The moment I set eyes on you, I knew we'd be good together. It's why I approved you."

Her whispered words build up the broken bits inside me almost instantly.

We're here because of me. She chose me. The words feel like a balm.

She leans in closer, rubbing her lips against mine, sending a jolt through my cock.

"I want you to make me cum with your tongue. And once you do that, I'll take care of you."

"I'd love to," I whisper right back.

She leads me to the bed and sits on the edge, grabbing a condom from the side. I suck in a breath as she rolls it over me. I have to hold it at the base for it to stop twitching in anticipation.

"Would you like me to help you with your heels or these," I point to the lingerie.

She smiles and shakes her head before lying straight on her back in the middle of the bed. As I'm getting between her legs, she commands again.

"Reverse."

Fuck! The thought of getting into 69 with her is heady. I can just imagine myself between her lips. Pumping.

I realize it's why she made me wear a condom.

I follow the command and hover over her. My weight resting on my arms and knees.

If I'm going to do this, I need to have her screaming.

Sucking in a deep breath, I lick her slit from one end to the other. The sound of her moan makes me lower my hips, wanting to graze her lips with my cock but she promptly holds me in place.

I place wet kisses all over her core before focusing on her peeking bud, taking it into my mouth, and sucking gently.

"Ahhh…"

Her moan grows louder, spurring me on. I spread her lips apart and start lapping at her insides, alternating between licking and sucking.

The taste of her is intoxicating. Sweet and salty, with a hint of something exotic and fresh.

My heart pounds in my ears as my mouth works to please her. Every muscle in my body is taut. I can't believe I'm actually doing this, touching her in this way.

Her body arches, her nails digging into the mattress. I can hear her rapid rapid, shallow gasps.

My cock is aching to be inside her mouth but since that can't happen, I penetrate her with my tongue.

The sound of her strangled whimper drives me wild and as I try to position myself at an angle so I can see her face, a big bomb drops on me.

Standing right by the wall, less than five feet away is Vanessa's husband–Julian. His face a mask. His eyes narrowed straight at me.

My heart drops to my stomach. My blood runs cold.

I gently tap her leg, whispering "Vanessa, he's here"

She hisses at me. "Did I give you the permission to stop?" The frustration in her voice is clear.

A shiver runs down my spine at the feeling of being caught. I notice Julian gently palming his cock.

My mind goes blank.

The next moment I'm inside Vanessa's warm mouth.

My eyes shut tight. I almost cum at the first touch.

Fuck!

I tighten my muscles and breathe through my mouth, trying to get my heartbeats to calm.

Her fingers grip the base of my cock, holding me steady as she slowly sucks on me.

Without hesitation, I focus on her cunt, determined to make her cum. I notice her strokes become more intense as she gets closer to her peak.

Soon, I'm hitting the back of her throat with the soft, swollen tip, and each time I do, she moans, sending vibrations through me.

Forgetting everything, I fuck her hard with my tongue. I want to cum in her mouth and want her to do the same.

Despite her husband hovering over us, I'm racing to my peak.

One hard hit against her throat. Another one.

Suddenly, my vision goes white.

As I come down from my high, I roll the condom off, tie the end, and throw it in a bin on the side.

Vanessa sprawls flat on the bed beside me, her chest heaving as she catches her breath. I can't resist leaning in, cupping one of her tits, and taking it in my mouth, tasting a hint of strawberry—maybe from her cream. My cock hardens again at the touch.

Before I can do more, a sharp crack lands on my ass cheek, making me jerk away. I glance at her, frowning, as she hisses, "Did I give you permission to do that?"

I open my mouth but just shake my head, swallowing my reply.

"We haven't set up any rules for punishment yet, but remember, you follow my commands, not your own urges."

She slowly lowers her hand, getting between my legs, palming my cock, stroking it with a satisfied hum as she feels me hard and ready.

Without a word, she reaches down and pulls a condom from beneath the edge of the mattress.

Her eyes, roaming over my body.

"Get on top of me," she orders, her voice firm yet sensual.

I quickly don the condom and position myself over her. She pulls me closer, her eyes fixed on mine, her expression demanding. The heat between us is palpable, and the intensity from earlier only seems to grow till she places her palms hard against my cheeks and pushes me inside her.

"Now don't hold back," she commands. "Give it to me as hard as you can."

I slowly start building pace. Keeping the thrusts hard. She gasps with each thrust. Her hands grip my hips, guiding my movements, her moans growing louder with every stroke.

Suddenly, she delivers a sharp spank to my ass, the sting making me gasp and thrust harder.

"Don't stop," she says, her voice is breathy "Keep going. I want to feel you lose control."

I try to maintain my rhythm, wanting her to cum with me but she smiles at me and grabbing me by the back of my neck, pulls me in for a kiss.

The lingering taste of red wine is intoxicating as her tongue plays with mine, sending another wave of arousal through me.

I try to hold back, but as she starts sucking my tongue, I cum with a shudder.

Shit! She didn't reach her peak.

Another wave of shame washes over me. Pulling out of her, I flop to the side and close my eyes.

Damnit!

Taking a deep breath, I turn to her and murmur, "I didn't realize…" Before I make another mistake, I ask, "Would you like me to wait a few minutes or should I continue with my fingers? I…"

She cuts me off with a kiss. This time it's deep, lingering, sweet. As she pulls away, her eyes hold a softness that I hadn't witnessed till now. But it's gone before I can react. She swiftly hops out of bed and walks into Julian's arms. Her heels are still on. The woman is sexy as hell.

"You know, Ethan, maybe you should consider seeing your wife with someone else more often," she says. "It could be a growth experience for you—a way to be truly free."

Julian, who's remained silent till now adds, "She's right. Sometimes seeing things from a different perspective can help you understand what you truly want."

I look between the two of them, grappling with their suggestion, unable to make sense. I nod, slowly slipping out of the bed.

"Thank you for the... experience," I manage to offer a smile, unsure how to react.

Vanessa offers a small smile. "You're welcome. Now, if you'll excuse me, I'd like to catch up on my sleep."

I walk back to my room, feeling strangely liberated. There's a deep sense of well-being rolling inside.

"Where were you?" Ava snaps the moment I step inside the room. The lights are all off except the two lamps on the side of the bed. She is standing by the window, a bathrobe wrapped around her.

Ignoring her, I step inside the bathroom and freshen up before heading to bed.

"At least tell me where you were, I was worried."

I hear the strain in her voice as I adjust the pillows behind me. I sit with my back propped against the headboard, eyeing her for a moment.

It's like a switch has flipped inside me.

"Drop the robe," I tell her.

"What? She frowns at me.

"Drop it," I command.

She quickly does as I ask. I regard her naked body before glancing at the semi I've been sporting.

"Did you enjoy being at the bottom today?" I ask her with a smirk and love how her gaze drops to the floor. "Now get over here and make me cum."

Her gaze lifts. There's confusion in it, but I don't miss the smile as she notices me hardening at the sight.

She settles on my legs and is about to impale herself on me when I hold her by the waist and give her another command. "Reverse."

Her insides are wet and takes me in easily. I hold her waist with one hand and the other one moves to her front, rubbing her clit.

Within minutes she is clenching around me, squeezing me hard.

As we eventually flop back in bed–tired, and sated, she leans into me, holding me tight.

"This… this was new," she breathes out. "What brought this on?"

I hesitate, wanting to keep the experience with Vanessa to myself. Details would be messy. "Just felt like a change."

She doesn't seem satisfied with the answer but doesn't question it and is soon out like a light.

I stay up until dawn, my mind tangled in the contrasts between Vanessa and Ava. Am I dominant or submissive? I don't have a clue.

And the truth is, I'm not sure which side of me I like more.

Chapter 4: Embracing Change

Ethan

I wake up lying flat on my stomach, body naked and Ava's soft fingers pushing the hair away from my face.

"Babe."

Her voice is soft and soothing and I instantly put my arms around her, pulling her close. She smells different. I frown and slowly pry my eyes open to find her naked body bending over, trying to wake me up. Her tits right in my face. I lean in and take one in my mouth and she giggles.

Something about that sound feels jarring. As the events of last night flood my mind, I pull away, my body stiffening as the memories solidify.

Julian's words run through my head.

"Sometimes seeing things from a different perspective can help you understand what you truly want."

I notice Ava fidgeting with her hair, unsure if she should sit next to me or not.

"They have a brunch set up in the gazebo if you'd like."

I hate the frown on her face; the hesitation in her voice. I want to be angry with her, but... I'm not.

"Have you eaten?" I ask slowly getting up.

"Not yet," she replies, her shoulders visibly relaxing.

"Okay. Give me ten minutes and we'll go together."

The mid-afternoon sun is blazing down as we step into the gazebo, but the mist fans, humming like bees, keep the air cool. There's a massive flower garden stretching out before us but all eyes are only on the people here. There's not a single bathrobe and only a few towels in sight. Most people are freely walking naked.

Everyone's hands are roaming over others except for the ones that are covered. I do get teased and palmed several times. I don't mind. It's great to feel wanted.

There's music playing and the vibe is all round great.

The brunch spread is lavish. Chilled champagne, smoked salmon, lobster mac and cheese, non-seasonal exotic fruits, cheese platters, and every sinful pastry imaginable.

Ava takes the corner table and picks at her plate like a nervous bird. I grab a pile and slide in beside her.

"You okay, babe?" I ask, keeping my voice low, as she leans into me.

She nods and I wonder if she's skittish because of me.

Before I can ask, Butch and Cassidy come over. In the background, I notice the other couple. The one from last night. They're smirking at Ava as if they now own a piece of her.

A surge of possessiveness washes over me, a primal urge to claim what I think I might be losing. But I shove it down, the hollowness inside me battling against this sudden resurgence of jealousy.

We're here to explore. I remind myself that once again.

"Want to try this?" I offer her a forkful of lobster, my voice strained. She hesitates for a moment, then forces a smile before leaning in.

"If you're up for another round with them or want to pick someone new, just let me know. No pressure, okay?"

Ava looks at me, her eyes thoughtful. "I think I'll pass for now."

"Alright," I say, nodding. "No big deal."

Post-brunch the crowd moves to the pool area. While some just lounge around with their partner, soaking up the sun, most others are in different stages of intimacy. Making out, fingering, masturbating, or having sex.

I have no interest in this hedonistic display. All I want is to find Vanessa and give in to what we started last night. But she's nowhere to be seen. Even Julien isn't around.

I wonder if she's like Cinderella who only comes out to play at night.

The sound of tick-tock, tick-tock echoes in my mind. Everyone's leaving tomorrow morning. We only have today.

We settle on empty lounge chairs. Ava is in my lap, my arms around her waist as we both take in the scene.

My eyes scan for Vanessa when a good-looking couple approaches us—Matt and Minnie. Good Will Hunting.

"You two seem like you're having a great time. First time here?" Minnie asks.

Ava sits up straight, her movements brushing against my cock. "Actually, yes. We just got accepted three days ago."

Matt laughs heartily. "Oh! So you're the ones who got pulled in with Oliver and Sophie."

Ava shifts in my lap again.

Minnie throws her hair back. "They're always looking for soft targets. I'm all for exploring kinks, but they pick one person and slowly try to convert them into their full-time slave." She makes a face and visibly shakes.

I pull Ava close, pressing kisses to her cheek, and rubbing her arm.

"So where are you from, if you don't mind my asking," I try changing the topic.

"Westchester," they both say together and I smile. This should be interesting.

I notice Matt mirroring my actions as he starts trailing kisses down Minnie's neck. His eyes are on Ava. Minnie's are on me.

I start fondling Ava's tits and Matt does the same. Minnie's tits are nothing in front of my wife's though.

In a hot minute, Minnie gets up from Matt's lap and leans in to start kissing Ava who enthusiastically responds.

"Wanna play?" I ask Ava, my voice low and she pulls away from the kiss.

"Do you?" She holds my gaze as she asks.

For some reason, this moment feels important in our dynamic. Do we find comfort in playing together or exploring individually?

I know Ava feels the same after last night.

"I'd love for you three to play for sure," I reply softly, "but for me, how about I play it by the ear? Works?" I ask Ava who considers my answer then nods, smiling.

Minne and Matt are game too, and soon the three of them are indulging. I watch while superficially participating through rubs and massages here and there. Ava does try to give attention to me too and this time the sight of Matt's cock inside her slick slit isn't as hurtful.

Maybe this little pinch of hurt is fine if I get to explore my own sexuality without the traditional norms.

Once they are done, we get inside the pool, take a few laps, and let our bodies cool down. As we're rinsing off under the showerhead right by the pool, I ask her to blow me.

Ava drops to her knees immediately and soon, right in front of thirty people, give or take, I'm roaring down her throat.

We take another shower out in the open before walking away. Instead of going back to the room, we walk around, exploring the mansion. The grounds are huge. We pick up a bottle of wine on our way back but Ava falls asleep within minutes of settling on the couch.

With no electronic devices, books, or any other source of distraction, all you can do is eat, drink, sleep, and fuck.

I transfer Ava to the bed, grab the bottle of wine, and decide to go looking for Vanessa. I can't not see her before leaving in the morning tomorrow.

The club room is locked.

They're not by the pool.

The terrace and most unoccupied rooms in the mansion are locked so I know they aren't there either.

My feet pick up speed as the sun starts coming down. I need to see her. Touch her.

Just as I'm taking a turn in the last section at the back of the mansion, I hear a laugh. A few steps and I'm smiling like a fool.

Sitting in the jacuzzi is the elusive couple. Vanessa and Julien.

Vanessa catches sight of me, a smile playing on her lips as she waves me over. "Hey, join us! The water's perfect."

Julien remains still behind his sunglasses, offering no visible reaction, but I sense no objection either.

I don't need a second invite.

"Would anyone like some sparkling wine?" I ask but Vanessa shakes her head.

"Maybe some other time?"

I nod and put the bottle aside before getting in the water.

This time there's not a stitch of fabric on her and I can't look away.

I foolishly try to sound intelligent by talking about the work I've been doing for one of the prominent magazines in the country along with the business I run.

Julien makes suitable noises, while Vanessa continues to play footsie with my cock. I squirm, gasp, and moan throughout. My arms are tight against the back of the jacuzzi for support.

The need to be possessed by her is all-consuming as she continues to laugh, her eyes twinkling with excitement, her lush body only partially visible in the water.

Julian doesn't say a word.

"I want you to eat me out," she suddenly announces before stepping out of the jacuzzi. There's a yoga mat nearby and she points me to lie down straight on my back.

As I get in position, she towers over me, watching me, before running her painted toes over my lips. Drops of water from her body keep dripping on me.

She plays with me for a bit before slowly kneeling down right above my face.

Her thighs are positioned on either side of my head and then she lowers herself. Her delicate sweet and salty taste fills my mouth and I lap it up, holding her in place so she doesn't move.

I know what she likes, so I start with that just that.

She rewards me with her moans and gasps that are throaty and much louder this time. While I continue focusing on her, somewhere in the background I hear a man grunting.

As Vanessa's body starts tensing, she lifts her hips slightly and not wanting to lose momentum, I use my fingers, quickly finding her g-spot and hitting it with my two fingers.

I'm guessing she is enjoying it because she grabs my hair tightly, staring at me as if possessed, her mouth open, her eyes wild, and her body ready to cum.

I increase the pace of my fingers, the sensation of my nails gently scraping her skin adding to the intensity. Vanessa's grip on my hair tightens, and with a final curl of my fingers, she screams, her body convulsing as she squirts on my face.

As her release continues, I hear shallow breaths and frantic grunts from the side. Turning my head slightly, I see Julien, his gaze fixed on us, masturbating with quick, urgent strokes. Within moments, he reaches his climax, his body tensing in the throes of his own release.

I'm in a bit of a daze as we get up but then we grab our belongings and head back to that clubroom and Vanessa hands me a condom before she asks me to take her from behind.

I know I'm distracted this time and supercharged, it's probably what explains me cumming once again before her. She brushes it aside and instead rewards me with a light kiss on my lips before leaning down and sucking on a soft spot on my neck.

I smile at her gesture. I wonder when we'll meet again.

As she pulls away, she whispers, "Thank you," in my ear before leading me to the door.

I'm almost back in my room in a happy high zone when I remember my bottle of wine.

If they're not going to drink it, then I'd rather take it. It's an expensive label and it'll be charged to my card so leaving it behind would be stupid.

As I walk back to the clubroom, the sight that greets me makes my heart drop.

Chapter 5: Re-evaluating Boundaries

Ethan

All of Vanessa's limbs are tied to individual chains hanging from the ceiling, her torso resting on the bed. Julien stands in front of her, one leg casually propped on the ottoman, his fingers tightly gripping her hair, forcing her to look at him.

"You did well today, my Dove. Exceptionally well."

I watch, frozen in place, my mind struggling to process what's unfolding before me.

"You even managed to move me enough to get off just by controlling him,"

Julien continues, his voice dripping with satisfaction. "I think my perfect little submissive has finally advanced to the next level."

Vanessa smiles, a twisted kind of pride in her eyes. "It's all for you, Leon. I live to please you."

A satisfied hum escapes him as he rubs his cock over her lips, taunting her before pulling back. "First, we need to reward you for what you did today. One for clearing your training and another for not cumming to his cock even once."

As I stand there, the puzzle pieces begin to fall into place, each one clicking together with certainty.

"Ask me for anything you want," Julien... Leon offers his tone almost tender. "Anything at all, and I'll make it happen."

Her voice trembles as she answers in a hushed whisper. "I want us to be official."

He chuckles. A sound that sends a shiver down my spine. "And?"

"What if we keep him?"

My heart slams against my chest as realization dawns. They're talking about me. I'm the "him" she wants to keep.

Julien's grip on her hair tightens just enough to make her wince before he kneels in front of her, brushing his lips against her cheek. "Once he's served his purpose, he becomes a trophy. You know you can't keep one."

"It's not like that, Leon. I…" she begins, but he silences her with a finger pressed to her lips.

"I promise I'll handpick the person for your next round."

My mind spins, the events of the past week racing through my head like a film on fast-forward. That meeting in the gallery. Julien's calculated silence, letting Vanessa take the lead. Was I chosen during our first meeting or was I just a convenient pick after we arrived? Was Ava getting caught up with the creeps a stroke of luck or again something orchestrated?

I take a deep breath as I glance back at them. Julien is now ruthlessly fucking her mouth, his grunts growing louder with each thrust, his fingers tangled in her hair as he tugs hard, his eyes wild with pleasure.

I can't watch anymore.

Turning away, I stumble back to my room, my thoughts a chaotic mess.

Why us? Or rather, me? Little clues keep surfacing in my mind, each one more disturbing than the last. The reason Leon never left the room. The dim lighting. The way Vanessa—no, Dove—never appeared in public.

The truth is undeniable. Leon's Grotto isn't about people exploring their desires. It's for Leon to explore his. And if others have some fun along the way, then that's just a bonus.

Ava is asleep when I get back. I lie down beside her, trying to calm my racing thoughts, but sleep eludes me.

First thing in the morning, I'm ready to leave.

"Ava, wake up," I gently shake my wife.

She stirs, blinking sleepily at me. "What's wrong?"

"We need to go," I reply, urgency threading through my voice as I hand her a robe.

"Right now?" She frowns, glancing at the window. "I thought we'd stay for breakfast."

"We'll beat the traffic if we leave now," I say, grasping for any excuse. "And I remembered I promised Doug I'd help with a project."

Ava studies me for a moment, her brow furrowed, before slowly nodding and getting up.

"Hey, what's this?" I sigh as her fingers trace the dark bruise on my neck. I'd noticed it in the mirror earlier—Dove's mark, a reminder of her claim on me.

I know she has sucked on harder, wanting for it to be unmissable.

Ava's eyes narrow slightly as she examines it, and I force a smile, trying to deflect her suspicion. "Just someone I ran into. It was dark... I didn't even get a good look at her."

The lie tastes bitter on my tongue. Not only had I seen Dove's face, but I'd also memorized every inch of her. My gorgeous, forbidden secret.

"How can you not know?"

I frown at Ava's tone.

"Freshen up and meet me at the outhouse. I'll settle the dues till then and keep the car running."

I leave before she can probe further, the mansion feeling suffocating as I make my way to the clubhouse. The heavy lock on the door, makes me sigh and walk away.

As we're on our way home, I feel gutted, knowing that I might never see Dove again. But deep down, I sense that this isn't the end. Two months later, fate presents another opportunity.

THE END

Dear reader,

Thank you for reading to the end! I hope the book lived up to your expectations!

Would you like to read part two? It's available at Amazon as well; just go to this book's product page or series page!

Exclusive erotic short story club

Want even more? You can join my exclusive erotic short club **for free**. By doing so, you will get a bunch of free stories (before I publish them on Amazon), audiobook coupon codes, and much more! Email me at amber.carden.books@gmail.com and I will send you a link!

Amber

© Copyright 2024 - All rights reserved.

The content contained within this book may not be reproduced, duplicated, or transmitted without direct written permission from the author or the publisher.

This book is copyright protected. It is only for personal use. You cannot amend, distribute, sell, use, quote or paraphrase any part, or the content within this book, without the consent of the author or publisher.

www.ingramcontent.com/pod-product-compliance
Lightning Source LLC
LaVergne TN
LVHW041631070526
838199LV00052B/3315